Audrey
the Aurora Bora elf

Spangle-Bangle
the star-hanging elf

Kenneth
the high-kicking elf

Betsy
the ball-throwing elf

Tilly-winkle
the doll-house elf

Bimble
the boat-building elf

Clodagh
the clock-watching elf

Dora
the droopy elf

Elvin
the extra-tired elf

Grandpa Elf

For Emma,
Happy Christmas! – M.S.

To super star Kayt,
Have a wonderful Christmas x – T.B.

Published in the UK by Scholastic, 2022
1 London Bridge, London, SE1 9BA
Scholastic Ireland, 89E Lagan Road, Dublin Industrial Estate, Glasnevin, Dublin, D11 HP5F

SCHOLASTIC and associated logos are trademarks and/or
registered trademarks of Scholastic Inc.

Text © Mark Sperring, 2022
Illustrations © Tim Budgen, 2022

The rights of Mark Sperring and Tim Budgen to be identified
as the author and illustrator of this work have been asserted
by them under the Copyright, Designs and Patents Act 1988.

ISBN 978 0 702313 59 2

A CIP catalogue record for this book is available from the British Library.

Printed in China
Paper made from wood grown in sustainable forests and other controlled sources.

1 3 5 7 9 10 8 6 4 2

This is a work of fiction. Names, characters, places, incidents and dialogues are
products of the author's imagination or are used fictitiously. Any resemblance to
actual people, living or dead, events or locales is entirely coincidental.

www.scholastic.co.uk

MARK SPERRING   TIM BUDGEN

20 ELVES at BEDTIME

SCHOLASTIC

The night before Christmas Eve,
Santa could NOT sleep.

So, a couple of his
reindeer chums said,

"You should count
some sheep!"

Now, Santa's counted sheep before
but something by the shelf

made Santa want to NOT count sheep,
and count gold buttoned . . .

Elves!

1. . . .

Here's a high-up elf who's reaching for a kite.

2 . . .

Here's a helpful elf
holding a ladder tight!

3...
Here's a beaming elf
with baubles yet to hang.

4...

Here's a rock star elf
who gave a toy a TWANG!

5...

Here's a ribboned elf
with all these gifts to wrap.

6...

Here's a

busy elf

– too busy

for a nap.

7...

Here's a little elf skipping through the snow.

8...

Here's a jingling elf with bells upon his toes.

9...

Here's a big, strong elf who's loading up a sleigh.

10...

Here's a kindly elf who gave Rudolph some hay.

11...

Here's an awestruck elf who glimpsed the Northern Lights.

12...

Here's a dazzling elf who hung a star so bright.

Yes, the night before Christmas Eve,
while counting elves, not sheep . . .

Santa sat down at his desk
and ALMOST fell asleep.

Yet, still, he kept on counting
lots of elves at work and play . . .

13 . . .

14 . . .

15...

And, there's still more on the way . . .

16...

Here's a weary elf who looked up at the clock.

17...

Here's a tired elf who downed her tools and STOPPED!

18...
Here's a sluggish
elf whose shoulders
dropped and drooped.

19...

Here's a tiny elf
who's feeling
EXTRA pooped.

20!

Here's a wise, old elf,
and this is what he said:

"With Christmas very,
nearly here, we ALL
should get to bed!"